Marla Frazee

In Every Life

Beach Lane Books • New York London Toronto Sydney New Delhi

For my grandson, Arthur

In 1998, during a service at All Saints Church in Pasadena, California, I heard a call-and-response version of a Jewish baby-naming blessing and immediately felt its potential as a picture book. The original source of the poem is unknown, but it has been adapted and used widely in welcoming ceremonies of all kinds. I've revised and attempted to illustrate the blessing many times over the ensuing years, with no luck. It wasn't until the fall of 2020, when so many things about our world were upended, that I felt it was time to try again. I hoped to capture and honor what we all have in common, no matter who we are or where we live. And, during the time I was working on it, my first grandchild was born. —M. F.

BEACH LANE BOOKS • An imprint of Simon & Schuster Children's Publishing Division • 1230 Avenue of the Americas, New York, New York 10020 • © 2023 by Marla Frazee • Book design by Marla Frazee © 2023 by Simon & Schuster, Inc. • Title type by Graham Bradley • All rights reserved, including the right of reproduction in whole or in part in any form. • BEACH LANE BOOKS and colophon are trademarks of Simon & Schuster, Inc. • For information about special discounts for bulk purchases, please contact Simon & Schuster Special Sales at 1-866-506-1949 or business@simonandschuster.com. • The Simon & Schuster Speakers Bureau can bring authors to your live event. For more information or to book an event, contact the Simon & Schuster Speakers Bureau at 1-866-248-3049 or visit our website at www.simonspeakers.com. • The text for this book is based on Goudy Handtooled and was hand lettered by Marla Frazee. •
The illustrations for this book were rendered in pencil and gouache on Strathmore 500 hot press paper.
Manufactured in China •1022 SCP
First Edition
2 4 6 8 10 9 7 5 3 1
Library of Congress Cataloging-in-Publication Data
Names: Frazee, Marla, author, illustrator. Title: In every life / Marla Frazee.
Description: First edition. | New York : Beach Lane Books, | [2023] | Audience: Ages 0-8 | Audience: Grades K-1 | Summary: A picture book celebrating both the highs and lows that everyone experiences in the course of a life. • Identifiers: LCCN 2022008098 (print) | LCCN 2022008099 (ebook) | ISBN 9781665912488 (hardcover) | ISBN 9781665912495 (ebook) • Subjects: LCSH: Life—Juvenile literature. | Experience—Juvenile literature. | Conduct of life—Juvenile literature. | Picture books for children. | CYAC: Life. | Conduct of life. | LCGFT: Picture books. • Classification: LCC PZ7.F866 In 2023 (print) | LCC PZ7.F866 (ebook) | DDC E] —dc23 •LC record available at https://lccn.loc.gov/2022008098 • LC ebook record available at https://lccn.loc.gov/2022008099

In every birth,

blessed is the wonder.

In every smile,

blessed is the light.

In every hope,

blessed is the doing.

In every sadness,

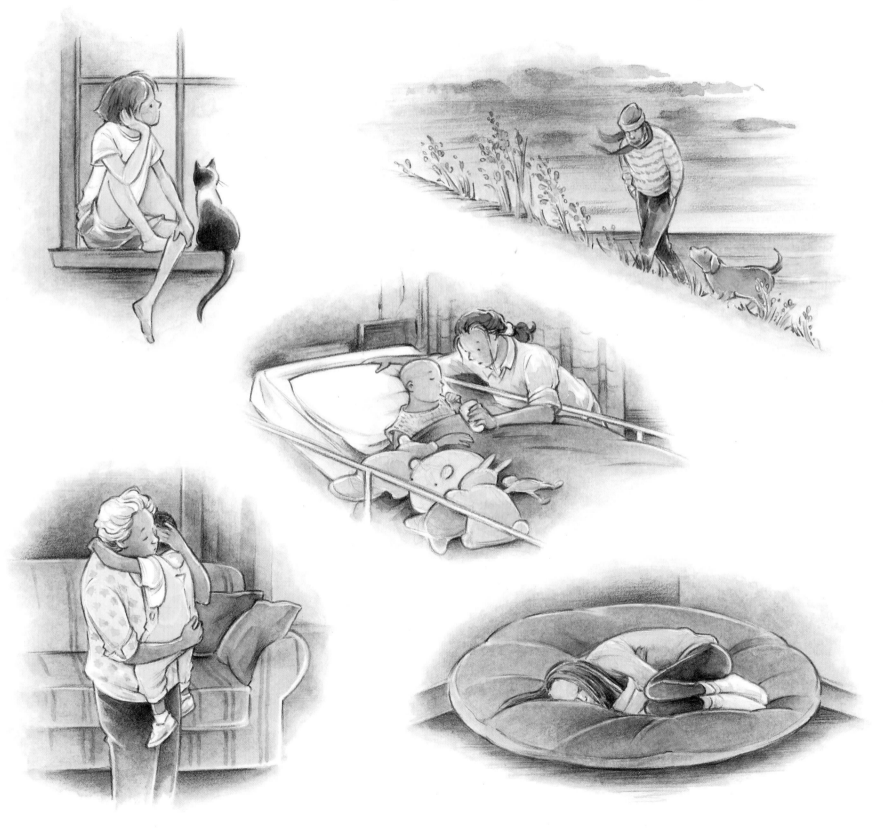

blessed is the comfort.

In every moment,

blessed is the mystery.

In every love,

blessed are the tears.

And in every life,

blessed is the love.

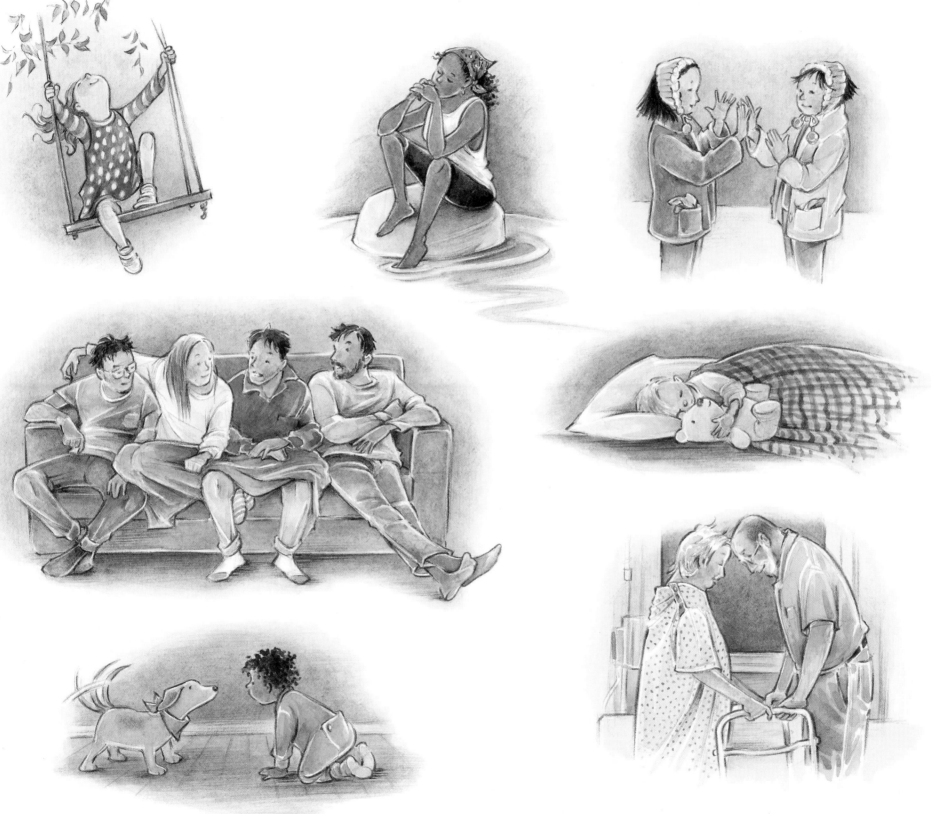

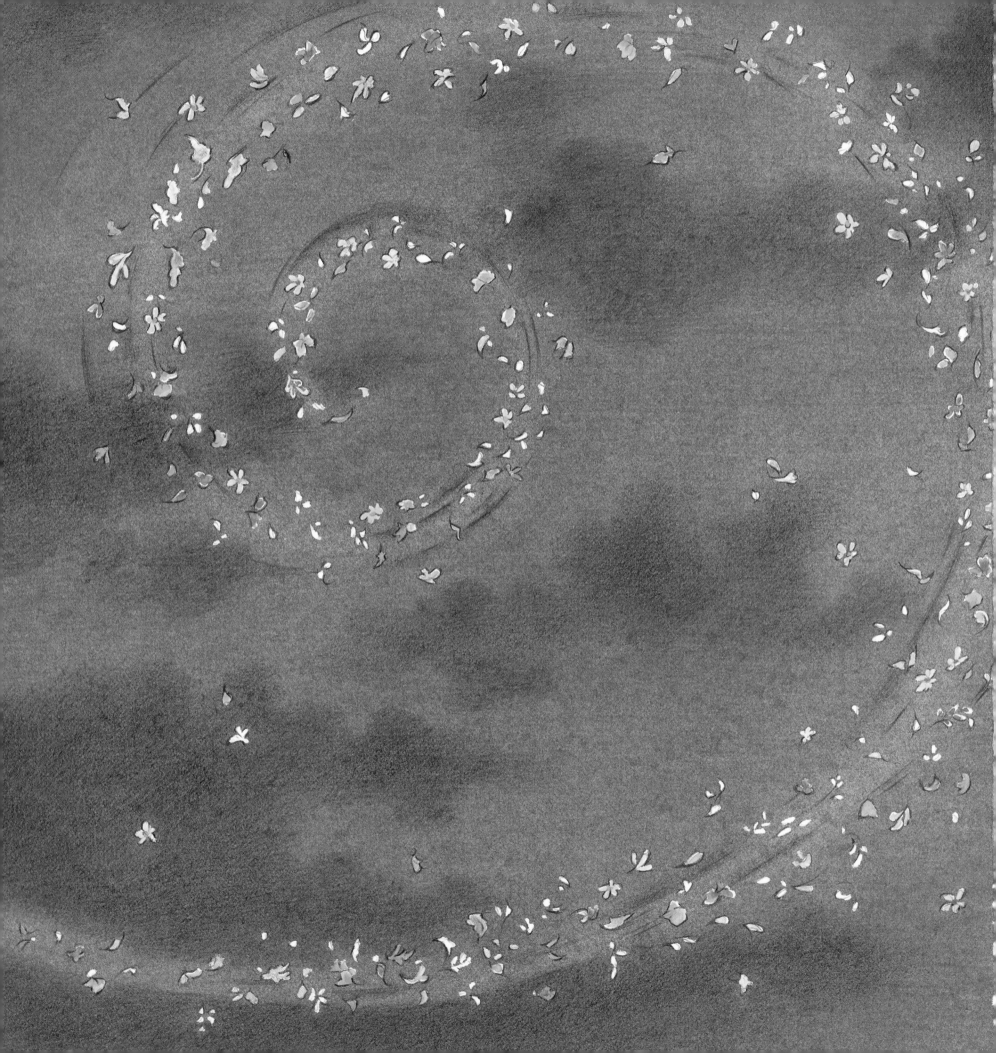